Mrs Goat
and her seven
little kids

A Red Fox Book

Published by Random House Children's Books
20 Vauxhall Bridge Road, London SW1V 2SA

A division of Random House UK Ltd
London Melbourne Sydney Auckland
Johannesburg and agencies throughout the world

First published in Great Britain by Andersen Press Limited 1990
Published in Australia by Century Hutchinson Pty. Ltd.

Copyright © Tony Ross 1990

Red Fox edition 1992
5 7 9 10 8 6

Printed in China

RANDOM HOUSE UK Limited Reg. No. 954009

ISBN 0 09 976900 X

Mrs Goat
and her seven
little kids

Tony Ross

RED FOX

Once upon a time, Big Mother Goat was about to go to
the supermarket.

"Kids," she said to her children, "don't you open that
door to ANYONE. If you do, the hungry wolf will
probably get in, and eat you all. Now, we don't want that,
do we?"

"No, we don't want that," said the kids.

"I'll kick him on the leg!" shouted the littlest one.

Now the wolf was hiding underneath the window, and he heard all this. When Big Mother Goat had gone on her way, he knocked on the door.

"Who's that?" shouted the kids together.

"I'm your mum," the wolf growled. "Open up the door, I forgot to give you your pocket money."

"You're not Mum," shouted the littlest one. "Mum's got a squeaky little voice that sounds like music."

"You're the Hungry Wolf," shouted the kids, and they wouldn't open the door.

So the wolf ran off to the music teacher's house.

"Teach me to speak in a squeaky little voice, like music," he growled. "If you don't, I'll bite your beak off."

"Very well," said the music teacher, and she did her best.

Then the wolf hurried back to the kids' house, and banged on the door. "Let me in, this is Mummy, I've got some sweets for you," he called.

"Show us your hoof first," said the littlest one, and the wolf pushed his paw through the letterbox.

"That's not Mum's hoof," cried the kids. "Mum's hoof's white. You're the Hungry Wolf."

The littlest one hit the paw with his little hammer, and the kids refused to open the door.

"OWWWWWWCHHHH!" The wolf snatched his paw out of the letterbox, and sucked his fingers. "White, is it?" he snarled, and went off to find an artist.

"It's got to be white, with a little black bit at the end, just like a goat's hoof," he told the artist. "Make a good job of it, and I'll not bite your nose off."

The artist made a very good job of it, and the wolf hurried back to the house where the kids lived.

He banged on the door, and shouted in a squeaky little voice, like music, "Let me in, dearies. I've brought you some comics from the supermarket." The wolf waved his paw through the letterbox. "Look, it's Mummy."

"It's Mum's hoof all right," said one of the kids.

"And it's Mum's little squeaky voice like music," said another. "Open the door."

"Not so fast…" said the littlest one. "Let's see your tail."

The wolf stuck his tail through the letterbox.

"Mum's tail is dainty, like an ear of wheat," said one kid. "This tail is grey and bushy, like…like…."

"Like the Hungry Wolf's tail," cried the littlest one. "Excuse me while I bite it."

The wolf howled, and the kids refused to open the door.

"So Mum's tail is dainty, like an ear of wheat, is it?" muttered the wolf, and he rushed off to see the dentist.

"I don't usually remove tails," said the dentist.

"If you don't remove this one, I'll bite your tail off," said the wolf.

"Then I'll make an exception in your case," said the dentist. "After all, I do have the necessary equipment. This'll not hurt."

The wolf stuck an ear of wheat where his tail was, and once again banged on the kids' front door.

"Let me in," he cried, in his little squeaky voice like music, waving his paw painted like a hoof. "I'm Mummy, and I've got ice cream."

He turned round, and wiggled his new tail.

"It's Mum's little voice, squeaky, like music," said one kid.

"It's Mum's hoof, white with a little black tip," said another.

"It's Mum's tail, dainty, like an ear of wheat," said a third.

"It's Mum!" they all shouted joyfully, and threw open the door. All that is, except the littlest one, who wasn't so sure, so he hopped into the coal bucket to hide.

In leaped the wolf, and swallowed six little kids whole.

"I thought there were seven," grumbled the wolf. "Seven would have been delicious. Still, six is okay."

So saying, he loosened his belt, and helped himself to a glass of Big Mother Goat's best beer.

The wolf took the beer into the back garden, and sat down in a wicker chair. Then, with an awful grin on his face, he dozed in the sun.

When Big Mother Goat got home, she was laden down with seven bags of sweets, seven comics, and seven ice creams.

The littlest one jumped out of the coal bucket, and told his mother exactly what had happened.

"He's still here, Mum," he bleated. "He's in the garden. He's in your chair."

"WHAT?" roared Big Mother Goat, dropping all her bags. "In my chair? With my kids in him? LET ME GET AT HIM!"

Big Mother Goat hit the dozing wolf at ninety miles an hour.

She butted him right out of the wicker chair.

She butted him so hard, that one of her kids shot out of his mouth.

She butted him again, and out came another.

"Not again!" pleaded the wolf, trying to crawl away. "Not on my bottom, my tail place still hurts…OW!"

She butted him again, and out flew a third kid.

Altogether, Big Mother Goat butted the wolf seven times. Once each to get back her six swallowed children, and once to send the wolf right over the trees, and away for ever.

Then she gathered her kids around her, dried their tears, and gave each one a big kiss on the nose...

and a slap on the ear for opening the door to a wolf.

Some bestselling Red Fox picture books

THE BIG ALFIE AND ANNIE ROSE STORYBOOK
by Shirley Hughes
OLD BEAR
by Jane Hissey
OI! GET OFF OUR TRAIN
by John Burningham
DON'T DO THAT!
by Tony Ross
NOT NOW, BERNARD
by David McKee
ALL JOIN IN
by Quentin Blake
THE WHALES' SONG
by Gary Blythe and Dyan Sheldon
JESUS' CHRISTMAS PARTY
by Nicholas Allan
THE PATCHWORK CAT
by Nicola Bayley and William Mayne
WILLY AND HUGH
by Anthony Browne
THE WINTER HEDGEHOG
by Ann and Reg Cartwright
A DARK, DARK TALE
by Ruth Brown
HARRY, THE DIRTY DOG
by Gene Zion and Margaret Bloy Graham
DR XARGLE'S BOOK OF EARTHLETS
by Jeanne Willis and Tony Ross
WHERE'S THE BABY?
by Pat Hutchins